All the Lights in the Night

ARTHUR A. LEVINE

pictures by JAMES E. RANSOME

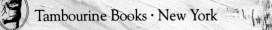

Tambourine Books · New York

In loving memory of my grandpa, Myron Shube.
And for Tony, my light.
—A.A.L.

To Lesa.
—J.E.R.

Library of Congress Cataloging-in-Publication Data
Levine, Arthur A., 1962–All the lights in the night/by Arthur A. Levine;
pictures by James E. Ransome. p.cm.
Summary: Moses and his little brother Benjamin find a way to
celebrate Hanukkah during their dangerous emigration to Palestine.
ISBN 0-688-10107-0 (trade)—ISBN 0-688-10108-9 (lib.)
[1. Hanukkah—Fiction. 2. Jews—Fiction. 3. Brothers—Fiction.
4. Emigration and immigration—Fiction.] I. Ransome, James, ill.
II. Title. PZ7.L57824A1 1991 [E]—dc20 90-47496 CIP AC
10 9 8 7 6 5 4 3 2 1
First Edition

It was a few days before Hanukkah in the town of Drahitchen. In the old days menorahs would have been taken out and polished for the holiday lights. Children would have been sent for the last onions or eggs for potato pancakes. But it wasn't the old days.

Just the other night, Russian soldiers had run through the town breaking windows and causing trouble. The tsar was spreading word that the Jews were responsible for the poverty of the country, and people believed him. Last week Mr. Shube, the tailor, had been forced to move in with Moses Kaplan's family when his house was burned down. And the ugly mood showed no signs of going away.

Mama went over to the shelf and took something down. Then she pulled the boys together. "I want you to take this lamp," she said. "It was your grandmother's, and it has enough oil for one night. Light it on the first night of Hanukkah and pretend it's a menorah. Then at least you'll be able to say the blessings once."

The small brass lamp was tarnished and dented. But still Mama cried as she stuffed it into the bag. Then she led them to the door where Papa was waiting with Mr. Morozov, the potato seller. The kind peasant had agreed to give them a ride in his cart to the station many miles away in Minsk, where they would take the train to the big city of Warsaw.

Moses tried to be brave, but everyone was crying and waving as the potato cart pulled away into the pink skies of dawn.

As the day wore on the two boys rumbled along, listening to the rattle of the potatoes and watching the clouds. "That cloud looks like Potemkin, the butcher," said Moses. "What do you think that one looks like?"

"Mama," sniffed Benjamin. Then he started to cry again.

Suddenly Mr. Morozov shouted back to the boys. "Cover yourselves! I think I see soldiers." Quickly Moses covered Benjamin with potatoes; then he buried himself. Shortly they heard Mr. Morozov whistling a tune as several horses approached.

"Good day, officer," Mr. Morozov said.

"Off to the market, old man?" asked the soldier.

"That's right," said Mr. Morozov.

"Well, get on with you, then!" the soldier said. Then he slapped Mr. Morozov's horse so that it whinnied and the soldiers laughed.

"I'll just take a potato for the road, old man," said the soldier. His hand came down a foot from Moses' head. Moses tried with all his might to keep his knees from shaking. Finally he heard the soldiers' laughter fade into the clomp of their horses riding away. Then he let out his breath in one long whistle.

Benjamin could not be calmed down, even when they stopped for the night at a farmer friend of Mr. Morozov's. But when the old man had settled the boys into a warm corner of the barn, Moses had an idea.

"Let's have Hanukkah a little early," he said, taking out the lamp.

"Mama said we only had enough for one night's worth," Benjamin warned.

"And tonight's the night!" Moses said. Together they said the blessings and watched the plucky little flame cast light here and there like gold coins.

"Tell me the story," whispered Benjamin. Moses knew he meant the story of Hanukkah. Papa always told it to them on the first night.

Moses took a deep breath. "Years and years ago, in the land of Judea, all the Jews lived peaceful lives. They worked and prayed and kept the holy lamp lit for God. But then one day an evil king named Antiochus came and tried to make them give up their religion. His soldiers bullied everyone and made a wreck of the temple. They even put out the holy lamp. No one knew what to do until Mattathias and his son Judah the Maccabee got everyone to fight back.

"They fought from hiding places in the mountains and somehow they beat Antiochus and his great big army. The next step was to clean the temple and relight the holy lamp. But they could only find enough oil to last for one night.

"Still, they said the prayers and lit the flame and that's when the miracle happened: That one little flask of oil, which was supposed to sputter out, kept on and on, burning brighter and brighter, until it had given the people light for eight days and nights."

Moses looked over at his brother. Usually, if Papa changed one word of the story Benjamin piped in with a correction. And Moses was sure he'd said a few things differently. But Benjamin was fast asleep, with his head on the blue scarf. The lamp made dancing shadows on his reddish hair—shadows that looked a bit like soldiers to Moses as he lay back on his bag. Their dark forms shrank and stretched at him until his eyes finally closed.

The next day Mr. Morozov dropped the boys at the station. On the train to Warsaw the conductor eyed them suspiciously. "Do you little boys have tickets?" he asked. But Moses had them right in his pocket.

After that they watched the farms and countryside rush by, and when Benjamin got homesick Moses told him stories, especially the story of Hanukkah. When it got to be dark on the train the boys secretly took out their grandmother's lamp. Moses thought the oil had burned out the night before, but somehow there was still some left. They stared wide-eyed at the cone of light, remembering games of dreidel and potato pancakes.

When they got to Warsaw both boys were shocked at how big everything was. They loved the fact that the streets were paved, and sang songs to the clicking sound their shoes made on the stones.

Moses had been told to find a place called the British Embassy, but by the time they found it, the sun had set. The office had closed for the night and other people were waiting in a line outside. Since tonight really was the first night of Hanukkah, Moses took out their lamp again. Once more, there seemed to be a tiny bit of oil left and this time the others joined in with their prayers. A ruddy-faced woman with a checkered shawl reminded Moses of Mama as she sang with her mouth wide open.

The next morning the boys waited to pay their money and get a set of papers that said they could enter Palestine. The man behind the counter didn't speak Moses' language, but Moses had practiced what he was supposed to say. When his turn came Moses' face was scrunched in concentration, but he said everything right. "Best o' luck, mate," said the man as he stamped their papers. Moses smiled. They were almost there.

But they still had far to go. Another long train trip awaited them, lasting several days. The people who traveled with them shared pieces of fruit and Moses and Benjamin shared their lamp. But by the time they reached the end of the trip they were sore and tired. And a boat ride still stretched between the boys and their brother.

At the docks Moses found a ship going to Palestine, and he paid the captain money for their tickets, saying the phrases he had memorized. But as he and Benjamin started up the plank, the big, bearded man hauled them back onto the dock.

"Where do you think you're going?" growled the captain.

"But I paid you for the tickets!" said Moses.

"Yeah? Well it's only enough for one of you. Which one will it be?"

Moses' stomach lurched. "Which one?" the man repeated slowly, pointing to each boy in turn.

Suddenly Moses remembered the lamp. "Here," Moses said to the man. "You can have this too. It belonged to my grandmother."

The captain looked at the battered lamp, then at the boys. "Well, maybe I can pass it off as an antique. All right, get on."

Moses and Benjamin scrambled into the crowded passenger area of the ship and sat gratefully on their bags.

That night they crawled up onto the deck for a breath of fresh air.

"I'm sorry we lost our lamp. Now we have nothing to light for Hanukkah," Moses said to Benjamin. The two boys leaned over the rail and into the salty breeze.

Then Benjamin tilted his head back and grinned.

"What are you smiling at?" Moses asked.

"All the lights," Benjamin said. "We have all the lights in the night." Stars glittered everywhere—in the sky and again in the dark, flat sea.

Softly Moses began to sing the Hanukkah prayer and Benjamin joined in. And their voices took to the air like seabirds, their bright music carrying over the wind.